P9-BZU-729

RIDGEFIELD LIBRARY
472 MAIN STREET
RIDGEFIELD, CT 06877
(203) 438-2282
www.ridgefieldlibrary.org

AUG 29
2017

To my daughter (and all children)—
may you know you are loved
—M. G.

To all little ones learning of their roots
—M. A.

SALAAM
R E A D S

An imprint of Simon & Schuster Children's Publishing Division
1230 Avenue of the Americas, New York, New York 10020
Text copyright © 2017 by Mark Gonzales
Illustrations copyright © 2017 by Mehrdokht Amini
All rights reserved, including the right of reproduction in whole or in part in any form.
SALAAM READS is a trademark of Simon & Schuster, Inc.
For information about special discounts for bulk purchases, please contact Simon & Schuster Special Sales
at 1-866-506-1949 or business@simonandschuster.com.
The Simon & Schuster Speakers Bureau can bring authors to your live event. For more information or to book an event,
contact the Simon & Schuster Speakers Bureau at 1-866-248-3049 or visit our website at www.simonspeakers.com.
Book design by Laurent Linn
The text for this book was set in ITC Cerigo Std.
The illustrations for this book were rendered digitally.
Manufactured in China
0617 SCP
First Edition
2 4 6 8 10 9 7 5 3 1
Library of Congress Cataloging-in-Publication Data
Names: Gonzales, Mark, 1975– author.
Title: Yo soy Muslim / Mark Gonzales.
Description: New York : Simon & Schuster Books for Young Readers, [2017] |
Summary: A lyrical celebration of multiculturalism as a parent shares with a child the value of their heritage
and why it should be a source of pride, even when others disagree.
Identifiers: LCCN 2016023128 | ISBN 9781481489362 (hardcover) | ISBN 9781481489379 (eBook)
Subjects: | CYAC: Multiculturalism—Fiction. | Muslims—Fiction. | Mexicans—Fiction.
Classification: LCC PZ7.1.G653 Yo 2017 | DDC [E]—dc23
LC record available at https://lccn.loc.gov/2016023128

Yo Soy Muslim

A Father's Letter to His Daughter

Mark Gonzales

ILLUSTRATED BY Mehrdokht Amini

SALAAM
READS

New York London Toronto Sydney New Delhi

It has been said,
if you climb a tree
to the very top and laugh,
your smile will touch the sky.

If you stay there overnight,
you will learn to count stars like dreams.

Inside cities, where skyscrapers
cloud the view of everything above,
walk in the steel shadows,
remembering Mayan pyramids
that too lived amongst the heavens.

There are questions we all ask
when we are learning what it
means to be human.

Who invented my hands?
Why wasn't I born with wings?
And
does the moon ever get lonely?

There are questions this world will ask.
What are you?
And
where are you from?

And there will come a day
when some people in the world
will not smile at you.

On that day
tell them this:

Yo soy Muslim.
I am from Allah, angels,
  and a place almost as old as time.

I speak Spanish, Arabic,
and dreams.

Mi mama creates life.

Mi abuelo worked the fields.
My ancestors did amazing things
and so will I.

No matter what they say,
　know you are wondrous.
A child of crescent moons,
a builder of mosques,
a descendant of brilliance,
an ancestor in training.

Say it with me:

Yo soy Muslim.

Our prayers were here before any borders were.

Yo soy Muslim,
and the deserts hold the secrets of souls.

Yo soy Muslim.
Hummingbirds send blessings with their wings.

Yo soy Muslim.
If you listen closely to the drum,
you can hear God.

Dance. Smile.
Laugh. Pray.
Say it with me:

Yo soy Muslim.
Yo soy Muslim.

By those who dance with the wind,
smile at the sun,
laugh in the rain,

and pray.